The Ladybird Key Words Reading Scheme is based on these commonly used words. Those used most often in the English language are introduced first—with other words of popular appeal to children. All the Key Words list is covered in the early books, and the later titles use further word lists to develop full reading fluency. The total number of different words which will be learned in the complete reading scheme is nearly two thousand. The gradual introduction of these words, frequent repetition and complete 'carry-over' from book to book, will ensure rapid learning.

The full-colour illustrations have been designed to create a desirable attitude towards learning—by making every child *eager* to read each title. Thus this attractive reading scheme embraces not only the latest findings in word frequency, but also the natural interests and activities of happy children.

Each book contains a list of the new words introduced.

W. MURRAY, *the author of the Ladybird Key Words Reading Scheme, is an experienced head-master, author and lecturer on the teaching of reading. He is co-author, with J. McNally, of 'Key Words to Literacy'—a teacher's book published by The Schoolmaster Publishing Co. Ltd.*

For use in schools, colourful work books, supporting material and apparatus based on Key Words is available. Write for details from the publishers:
WILLS & HEPWORTH LTD., LOUGHBOROUGH, Leics.

THE LADYBIRD KEY WORDS READING SCHEME has 12 graded books in each of its three series—**'a'**, **'b'** and **'c'**. These 36 graded books are all written on a controlled vocabulary, and take the learner from the earliest stages of reading to reading fluency.

The **'a'** series gradually introduces and repeats new words. The parallel **'b'** series gives the needed further repetition of these words at each stage, but in different context and with different illustrations.

The **'c'** series is also parallel to the **'a'** series, and supplies the necessary link with writing and phonic training.

An illustrated booklet—' Notes for Teachers ' —can be obtained free from the publishers. This booklet fully explains the Key Words principle and the Ladybird Key Words Reading Scheme. It also includes information on the reading books, work books and apparatus available, and such details as the vocabulary loading and reading ages of all books.

Book 5a

THE LADYBIRD KEY WORDS
READING SCHEME

Where we go

by

W. MURRAY

with illustrations by

JOHN BERRY

Publishers : Wills & Hepworth Ltd., Loughborough

First published 1964   Ⓒ   Printed in England

Jane, Peter, Mummy and Daddy all want to go for a walk.

"We will go up the hill," says Daddy. "Yes," says Peter, "let us go up the hill. It is fun up there."

Pat the dog wants to go. He jumps up and down. "Yes," says Peter to Pat, "you can come. You can come for a walk with us. You can come up the hill."

"No," says Jane to her cat. "You cannot come for a walk. You will be at home. You can have some milk."

"Come on," says Daddy. "Off we go. Off we go up the hill."

---

new words   walk   hill

Off they go. Peter walks with Daddy, and Jane walks with Mummy. They go by the houses and the shops. They see some cars and a bus. On they go to the hill.

"I like to go where there are trees and flowers," says Jane. "Where do you want to go, Peter?"

"I want to go where I can see rabbits and horses. I like to go by the farm," says Peter.

Daddy says, "Yes, we can go by the farm."

"Look," says Jane, "I can read where it says TO THE HILL."

"Yes," says Peter, "and I can read BUS STOP."

---

new words   by   where

Now they walk by the water. Pat wants to go into the water. Peter will not let him. "I want to look for fish," he says.

"I can see two down there," says Jane. "Look, Peter, can you see a big one and a little one?"

"Where?" says Peter. Then he says, "Yes, I can see them. I can see them now."

Mummy and Daddy go on. They are by the trees. "I can see the hill now," says Mummy. Daddy looks for the children. "Come on," he says. "We will go on to the farm. We can get some milk there."

"Yes," says Mummy, "we will all have some milk."

---

new words

now them

Mummy, Daddy and the children walk up to the farm. They go by the pigs. There are two big pigs and two little ones.

Jane likes the little pigs. She gives them some of her cake. Peter has some apples and he gives some of them to one of the big pigs. "This big pig likes apples," he says. "He wants all of them now."

"Where are Mummy and Daddy?" says Jane.

"They are by the cows," says Peter. "They want to get some milk for us. Come on, Jane, and have some milk now."

The two children walk to Mummy and Daddy. They want some milk.

---

new words

pigs   of

They all go in. "Here you are," says the man, "here is some milk for you." Jane and Peter and Mummy have some of the milk, and Daddy says, "Now I want some, please."

The man works on the farm and he likes to talk to them about it. He talks about the cows, and he talks about the pigs. He likes his work.

Then Daddy talks to the man about the walk. He says where they want to go. "Yes," says the man, "I like to walk up the hill. I like to be up there. You can see the sea."

He gives Pat some milk.

---

new words   talk   about

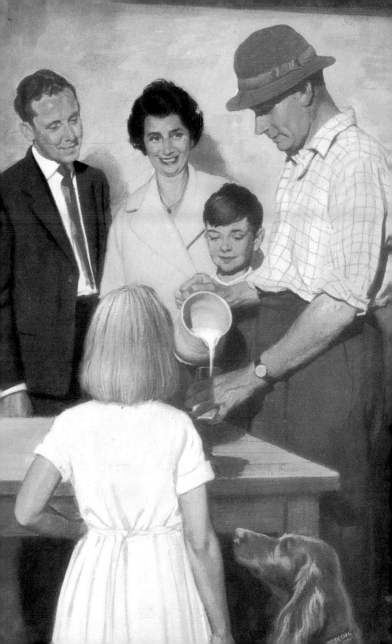

They can see the top now. They can see the top of the hill.

"We will stop at the top to eat," says Daddy. "Yes," says Peter, "let us walk to the top and then eat. We all want to eat."

"Look," says Jane, "I can see DANGER." "Yes," says Daddy, "do not go there."

Mummy says "Can you see the train?" "Yes," says Jane, "I can see it down there. It looks like a toy train."

"Look at the little houses," says Peter. "It is fun to see them like this. Now I can see the farm." The children talk about the farm.

new words

top   eat

Here they are in the sun at the top of the hill. Mummy, Daddy and the children all like the sun. They stop now to look down the hill.

They can see the farm and a man with some cows. The cows are going to the water by the trees. A little red car is going to the farm. The train is going to the station.

" Look," says Jane, " I can see the sea. I can see the sun on the sea."

" Yes," says Peter, " I can see it. I can see the sea. There is a boat on it."

The children like to talk about the sea.

new words   sun   going

There are trees at the top of the hill. Daddy says, " Now we will eat by this tree." Jane and Peter help Mummy, and then they all sit down to eat.

Daddy wants to sit by the tree. Mummy and the children like to be in the sun. Pat sits with them. They all sit where they can look down the hill.

Daddy talks about the afternoon. He says, "We are going to play in the sun this afternoon, and then we are going to walk down the hill for tea."

" Good," says Peter, " it will be fun to play with Daddy this afternoon."

---

new words   sit   afternoon

It is the afternoon. Daddy, Mummy, Jane and Peter sit in the sun at the top of the hill. Pat wants to eat. The children talk about the games they like.

Then Peter says to Daddy, "Are you going to play with us this afternoon? You said so." "Yes," says Jane, "you said so."

"Yes," says Daddy, "I said it, so I will play. What do you want to play?"

"Let us play with the ball," says Peter. Jane says, "Yes, that will be good fun."

Daddy and Jane have the ball. Peter wants to get it, and Daddy and Jane have to stop him.

---

new words   said   so

Now they are all going down the hill. Mummy says, "I like to sit in the sun for the afternoon."

Pat runs on. "What can the dog see?" says Daddy. "He can see rabbits," says Peter. They all look at the dog.

"Yes, they are rabbits," says Peter. "I said so. Look, he is going after them."

"Run after him, Peter," says Mummy. "Get him, Jane."

Pat runs after the rabbits, and Peter runs after Pat. Jane says, "Stop, Pat. Come here. Be a good dog and come here." Pat runs on. Peter cannot get him.

Then the rabbits go down. Pat cannot get at them now.

---

new words   run   after

Down go the rabbits, so that the dog cannot get them. Pat wants to go down after them.

"Look, he is going down after the rabbits now," says Jane. "Pull him out, Peter. Pull him out, please." "Yes," says Mummy, " pull him out now, Peter."

Peter pulls and pulls at Pat. "Here he comes," says Jane. "Good for you, Peter."

Now Pat is out. He runs away. "Let him go," says Daddy, " he will come after us. We have to go on now."

The afternoon sun is going down. Mummy says she wants some tea. They walk on down the hill. Pat comes after them.

new words

pull   out

The children talk about the dog and the rabbits. "It was good of you to pull Pat out," says Jane to Peter.

"I must have some tea after that," says Peter. "Yes, we are going to have some tea now," says Jane, "Daddy said so."

Here they are at a tea shop. "It says AFTERNOON TEAS," says Jane. "I can read it."

"Let us go in and sit down out of the sun," says Peter. "I want to eat." "Yes," says Mummy, "we can eat here, but what about the dog?"

"He can come in," says Daddy, "but he must be a good dog."

"Yes," says Jane to Pat. "You must be a good dog."

new words   must   but

In they go. "You must be a good dog," says Jane to Pat. "You must sit here by my chair and not run about."

Daddy pulls out a chair for Mummy. Peter sits on a little chair, and Daddy has a big chair.

"What are we going to eat?" asks Daddy. "I must have some tea, but I do not want to eat," says Mummy.

"Can I have some cake, please?" asks Peter. "Can I have some milk, please?" asks Jane.

The girl comes up to them, and Daddy asks her for tea and milk and cakes. After this they all talk about the afternoon. "It was a good game at the top of the hill," says Peter.

new words chair asks

After they have had tea Jane and Peter see a boy and a girl come into the tea shop. "Look," says Jane, "they go to our school. We must talk to them."

"Can we talk to them now, please?" Peter asks Daddy. "Yes," he says, "but let Pat sit here by my chair."

Jane and Peter go to talk to the boy and girl. They pull out chairs and sit down. "We have had our tea," says Peter.

They talk about the afternoon walk to the top of the hill. Then they talk about school.

Pat runs to Jane. "No, Pat," she says, "you are not going to run about in here. Daddy said so."

---

new words   **had   our**

Daddy gets up from his chair. "We have had our tea and now we must go," he says. "We will walk to the station and go home by train." The children like this.

They go out from the shop and walk down the street. In the street the children look in the sweet shops and the toy shops, but they do not stop. Pat pulls Jane after him.

Peter asks Daddy where the station is. "It is in this street," says Daddy. "On you go, and do not let the dog run away from you."

The children want to get to the station. They like to go by train.

new words   from street

The children soon come to the station. They go in from the street.

As they go in, a big train pulls out from the station. They look as it is going by.

"It is a goods train," says Peter, "and there are pigs and cows on it."

Pat wants to run after it, but Jane will not let him. "Keep by me," she says to her dog, "you must not run after the train."

As Mummy and Daddy come up, Jane asks, "Where is our train?" "It will be here soon," says Daddy, "the man said so."

Then the train comes in. "Come on," says Mummy, "let us get in. We will soon be home."

---

new words   soon   as

As soon as they sit down in the train the children look out of the window. From the window they can see more and more streets and houses going by.

"Now we can see the hill where we had our walk," says Jane. "Look out of the window, Mummy, you can see more now. You can see the top of the hill. I can see where we had our game."

"Can you see the farm, Jane?" asks Peter. "Yes," she says, "there are some cows by the farm house, and some more cows by the pigs."

"Now I can see where you had to pull Pat away from the rabbits," she says.

---

new words   window   more

Who is the other man in the train? He is from the farm, and he talks to Daddy about it.

Who is the girl with Jane? The man from the farm is her Daddy.

Who is the other boy? He is from Peter's school. He eats an apple. He has some more apples and gives one to Jane, one to Peter, and one to the other girl.

Jane and Peter talk to the boy and girl about the walk they have had. The girl asks Jane to come to tea at the farm.

As Daddy looks out of the window he says, "We will soon come to our station."

new words

who   other

As the train stops, Peter looks out of the window. "Which station is this?" he asks. "Yes, which is it?" asks Jane.

"It is our station," says Daddy. "We get out here. Get the bags. Which are our bags?"

Mummy gets her bag. Daddy has the other. Then they all get out.

Jane talks to the other girl, who helps her with Pat. "Thank you," she says.

They go from the station to the street as soon as they can. "Pat wants to walk," says Jane. "Yes," says Mummy, "but we must get a bus."

"Let us sit on top of the bus," says Peter.

new words which bag

They walk down the street. "Which is our bus?" asks Peter. "Which is it?" he asks again. "Not this one, the other one," says Mummy. She asks Peter to take the dog into the bus.

But Pat will not get on. He wants to run away.

"You must get on," says Peter. "Here comes Daddy," says Jane from the window, "he will help."

Daddy helps Mummy on to the bus. Then Peter takes the bag from Daddy, as Daddy puts Pat on to the bus.

More boys who go to Peter's school get on. They talk to Peter about the game they have had.

new words

again   takes

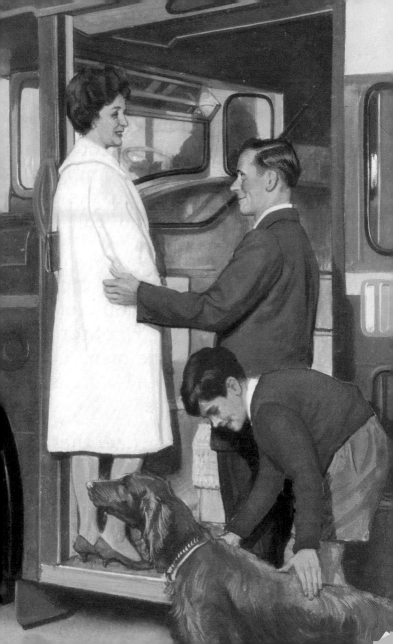

Jane and her brother are going down the street in the bus.

"Which bag has the sweets?" asks Jane, who wants to eat again. "The other one," says Mummy. As Jane takes out the sweets she gives her brother one. "You can have some more," she says.

Soon the bus stops by the Fire Station. Peter looks out of the window. "There is the Fire Station," he says. "I can see the men. Look! There go the firemen!" he says. "There must be a fire."

"Where there is fire there is danger," says Mummy. "I do not like it."

"The men will soon put out the fire," says Daddy.

new words   brother   men

Peter and his sister get off the bus to walk home. Soon they go by the school. "What do you like to do at school?" Jane asks her brother. "I like to read and draw," says Peter. "So do I," says his sister, "or I like to make things," she says.

"Look, Daddy is going to talk to that policeman," Peter says. "Yes," says Jane, "we know him, and we know his little boy who comes to our school."

Mummy talks to the men in the shop. She wants some things for the house. Peter takes the bags again to help Mummy. He and his sister want to go home now.

new words
sister   know

" Look," says Peter to his sister, " what is this?"

" Read all about it!" says the man. " Read all about it!"

Peter knows how to read. He reads " BIG FIRE THIS AFTERNOON."

" We saw the firemen go," says Jane to her brother. " We saw them from the bus. The men know how to put a fire out. They will have put it out by now."

Peter says to his sister, " I can read some more. Look, it says DANGER, MEN AT WORK." He reads it again to his Daddy, and Jane reads to her Mummy.

Daddy says " It is good that our children know how to read."

new words   how saw

DANGER
MEN
T WORK

BIG FIRE
THIS
AFTERNOON

BLAZE IN
VAREHOUSE MAY.

The two children are at home with Mummy and Daddy. Jane and Peter know they will soon have to go to bed.

"We saw how to milk cows," says Jane. "Yes," says Peter to his sister, "and we saw how the rabbits can jump. The man at the farm said we can go up there again. I want to see the horses again."

"The girl at the farm will soon ask us up to tea," says Jane to her brother. "Daddy will take us up by car. Then we can have fun."

"Come on," says Mummy, "I have to take you off to bed now. Up we go."

no new words